WHAT ON EARTH
IS UNDER MY BED?

BY LAURA QUINN   ILLUSTRATED BY KEVIN MC HUGH

What on earth
is under my bed?
I can sense something, oh, what dread.
Scared and frightened, that describes me,
But I will not rest,
until I see.

What on earth is under my bed?
It's a monster with a pumpkin head.

It has big bright eyes, teeth sharp and white,
I want to confront it but I might get a fright.

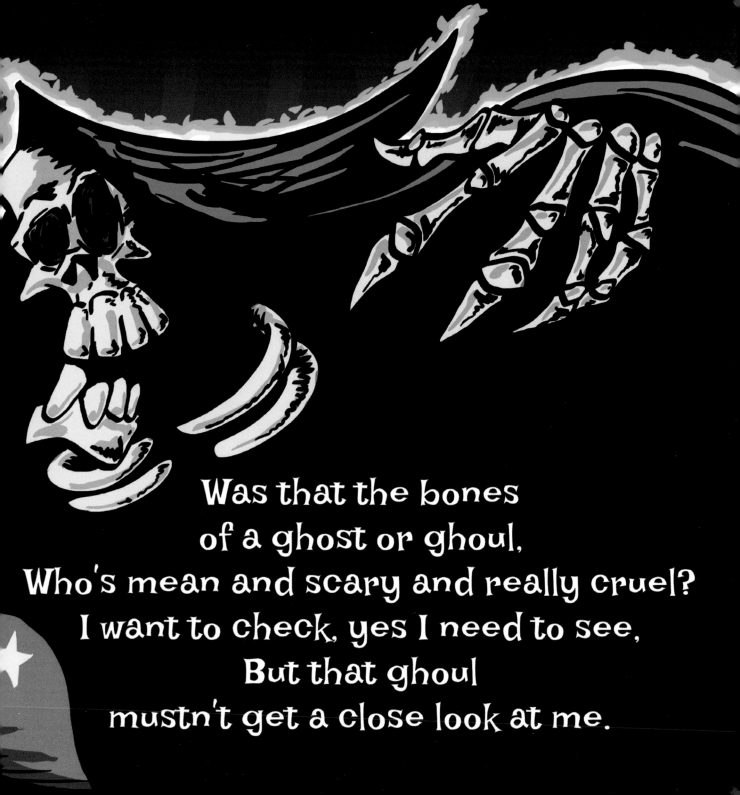

Was that the bones
of a ghost or ghoul,
Who's mean and scary and really cruel?
I want to check, yes I need to see,
But that ghoul
mustn't get a close look at me.

I've thought about it
even more,
I know what's on my bedroom floor.

Are they **big feet** that I spy?
I must be wrong,
I'll tell you why.

A fairy's feet would be tiny **and** small.
A ghost would not have,
feet at all.

Face painted white
and wearing a frown,
This must be a

Clumsy clown?

But I will stop
this guessing game,
Whatever it is,
it
has a name.

Though I'm as scared as I was before,
I won't sleep till I know for sure.

Here goes...
I won't change my mind.
I'll take a

quick peek,

seeeeeeee

what

I

find.

The creature's
lying awfully still.
Is something wrong?
Maybe it's ill?
I'll give it a poke with
my big toe,
To wake it up...
so then I'll know.

Mmmm,
that cry was gentle, the voice was weak,
Much softer than even a fairy would speak.
Wait a minute, do I see a hand,
On the floor, with fingers fanned?
OH NO,
This has to be a joke.
Sharp teeth? Gloves?
A long black cloak?
HUH!
A VAMPIRE!
What
will I do?

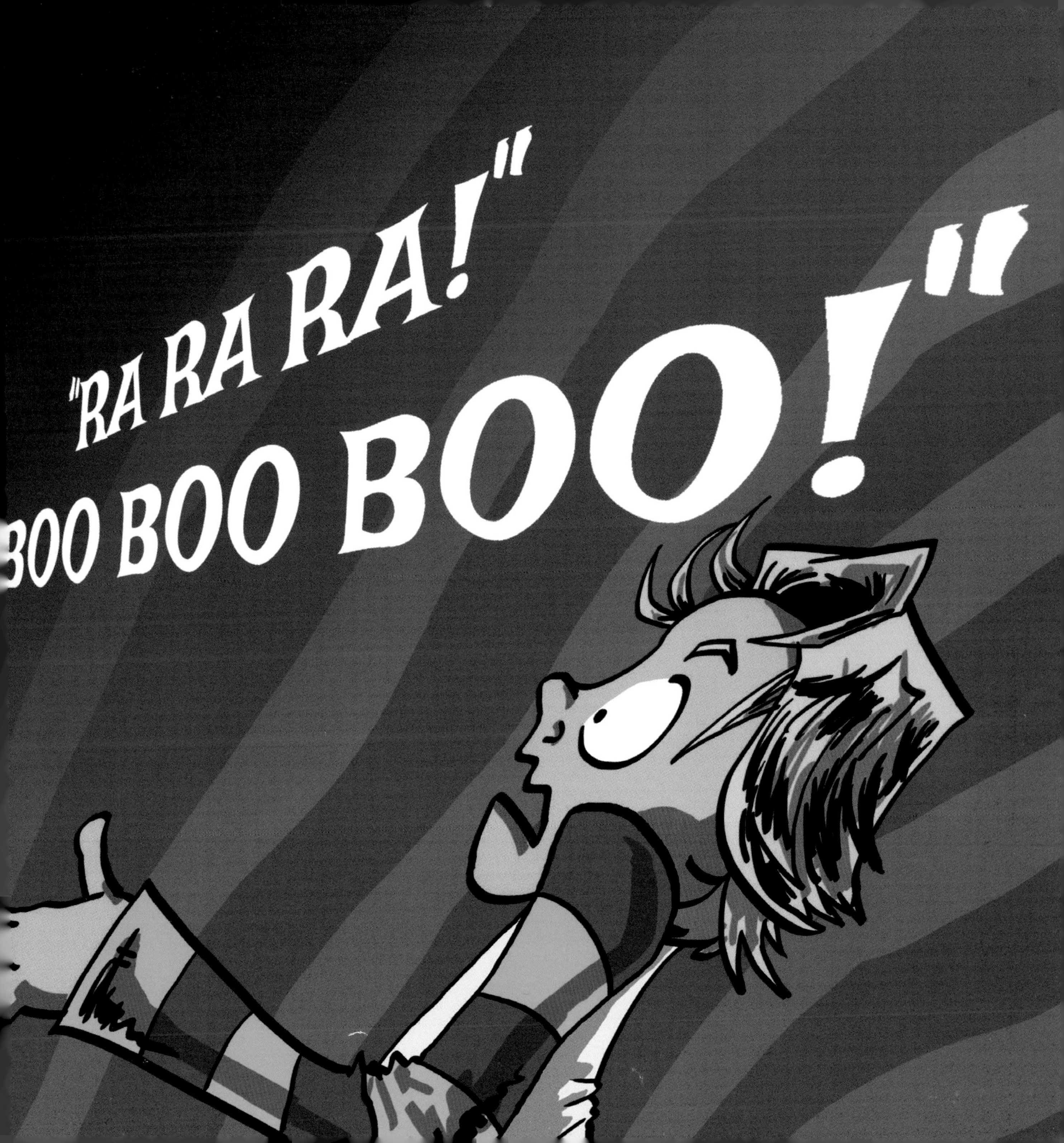
"RA RA RA!"
BOO BOO BOO!"

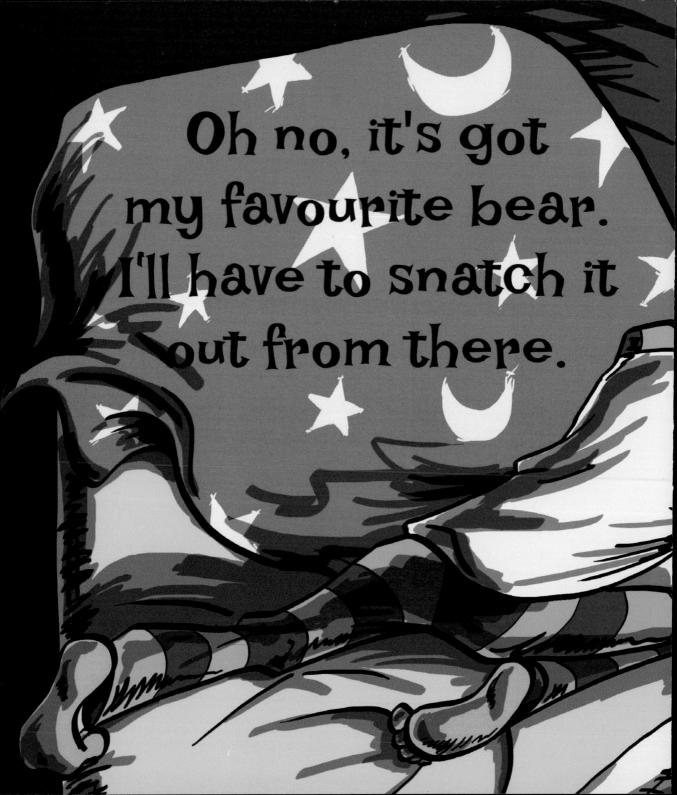

Slooowly

it crawls
from under the bed,

Yawning,

Stretching,

scratching its head.

I laugh out loud at what I see

"Is it morning?" my little brother cries?
He's tired,
weary,
rubbing his eyes.

Still In his Halloween costume,
with a sleepy head,
All this time,
it was

HE...
...who was...

under my bed.

To my son, Cián you are my world and my inspiration, I love you.
To my patient, loving, husband Peter, thank you for believing in me
and Monkey Blue.
To all my friends and family, there are too many to name
but you all know who you are.
Thank you,
you have ALL been an amazing encouragement in times of self doubt.
A special thank you to Karen McDermott from Serenity Press for
"getting the ball rolling."
To the Monkey Blue fans, thank you for loving him as much as I do.
Laura

To my wife, Jo, for making real life as colourful as my illustrations.

Kevin

Ghosts or Ghouls? Well, there's simply no such thing,
They don't exist, nor never will,
Nor does a Scary fairy or a wicked witch.
And as for vampires? They don't exist.
Monsters??? Well...they are made up too,
Only created to entertain you,
So always remember,
no matter what you "think" is out there,
They are all just pretend, to give you a scare.
So when you go to rest your head,
There's really no need
to check...

...under your bed.

Also by Laura Quinn

Monkey Blue Press
Enniskillen, Northern Ireland

First published by Monkey Blue Press in 2017
www.monkeybluepress.com

Laura Quinn (Quinn, Laura)
What on earth is under my bed?

ISBN 978-0-6481906-4-6 (sc)
ISBN 978-0-6481906-3-9 (hc)

Printed by The Print Factory, Enniskillen Tel: +44(0)28 66 325 325

Visit Laura Quinn: www.monkeybluepress.com
Visit Kevin McHugh: www.kevinmchughart.com

www.makingmagichappenacademy.com